GECKO is FRUSTRATED

A book about KEEPING CALM

Written by Sue Graves

Illustrated by Trevor Dunton

W

FRANKLIN WATTS

LONDON · SYDNEY

Gecko often got frustrated. He got frustrated when Mum said he couldn't have a biscuit before lunch. She said that was **the rule**!

But Gecko got cross. He stamped his feet and said it **wasn't fair**.

Gecko got frustrated at school.
He got frustrated waiting for Miss Bird
to **mark his work**.

He got frustrated when Rhino **took ages**
to choose a picture to colour.

Gecko got very frustrated doing sewing
in craft lessons. He made a real mess.
Miss Camel said he should **calm down**
and **take his time**.

Gecko got frustrated when Mum helped him **cross the road**. He said he could cross by himself. But Mum said it was **too dangerous**.

Gecko got frustrated at other times, too.

He got frustrated trying to button up his bag.

He **gave up**. He said it was **too hard**.

Gran said it was a good idea to keep trying.

But Gecko **didn't want to keep trying**.

He said buttons were very silly!

One day, Rhino came to play. He had a new jigsaw puzzle. Gecko liked doing puzzles.

Gecko told Rhino to be careful with all the pieces and put them in the **right place**. But Rhino didn't listen. Gecko got **frustrated**.

Soon the puzzle was almost finished. But there was one piece **missing**! Gecko got so frustrated that he **got cross** with Rhino.

He said it was Rhino's **fault**. He said Rhino had spoiled the puzzle. Rhino was upset.

Gecko **was sad** that he had upset Rhino.
He went to find Dad. He told Dad he wished
he didn't get so frustrated with everything.
Dad **listened carefully**.

Dad said when he was little, he used to get frustrated, too. He said when he was little, he couldn't tie knots. He got very frustrated.

But he didn't give up. He took a deep breath and **tried again, and again ... and again.** At last, he did it! He was very proud. Dad said it was a good idea to keep trying if you found something hard to do.

Dad said sometimes he felt frustrated if he had to wait his turn. He said he remembered to take a **deep breath** and to think of **something nice** while he was waiting.

Gecko had a think. He said he could do those things, too.

21

The next day at school, Miss Bird said that everyone had to make kites. She said the best kites would be hung up. She said everyone had to **cut out** the kites **carefully**. She said they had to **tie on** the string **carefully**, too.

Gecko cut out his kite carefully. He coloured it carefully. But it was hard to tie on the string. He started to feel **frustrated**. Then he remembered what Dad said. He took a **deep breath**.

He thought how nice it would be if Miss Bird chose his kite to hang up. Then he **tried again, and again ... and again**. At last, he tied on the string. Gecko was **proud**.

Miss Bird looked at all the kites. She chose lots of kites to hang up. Best of all, she chose Gecko's. She said she was **pleased** that Gecko **didn't give up** and kept trying.

Gecko said it was much better to **keep calm** and not get frustrated. He said it was much better to **keep trying**, too.

A note about sharing this book

The *Behaviour Matters* series has been developed
to provide a starting point for further discussion on
children's behaviour both in relation to themselves
and others. The series is set in the jungle with
animal characters reflecting typical behaviour
traits often seen in young children.

Gecko is Frustrated
This story looks at the importance of remaining
calm and being patient when faced with
frustrating situations and provides opportunities
to work out strategies for dealing with them.

How to use the book
The book is designed for adults to share with either
an individual child, or a group of children, and as a starting
point for discussion.

The book also provides visual support and repeated words and phrases
to build reading confidence.

Before reading the story
Choose a time to read when you and the children are relaxed and have
time to share the story.

Spend time looking at the illustrations and talk about what the book
might be about before reading it together.

Encourage children to employ a phonics first approach to tackling
new words by sounding the words out.

After reading, talk about the book with the children.

- Encourage the children to retell the story in their own words.

- Talk about the different situations that Gecko found frustrating. Do the children get frustrated about similar things? For example, do they feel cross when they are not allowed a snack too close to lunchtime? Encourage them to share their experiences with the others.

- Discuss the importance of waiting their turn when others in class need the teacher's help or when they want their work marked. Why do they think it is important to wait patiently in these situations? How would they feel if someone interrupted while the teacher was helping them or marking their work?

- Point out the part in the story where Rhino doesn't listen to Gecko. Ask the children if they feel frustrated when they are not listened to. Ask them to recall times when this has happened – how did they feel?

- Ask the children to talk about things they have found difficult to do or achieve. Can they recall a skill that they had to persevere with before getting it right, e.g. getting dressed, writing neatly, learning to swim?

- Invite each child to draw a 'before' and 'after' picture of something they found frustrating – either a skill or a situation – and how they overcame the problem. Ask them to label their pictures 'before' and 'after'.

- At the end of the session, invite the children to show their pictures to the others, and to explain how they overcame their frustration.

For Isabelle, William A, William G, George, Max, Emily, Leo, Caspar, Felix, Tabitha, Phoebe and Harry – S.G.

Franklin Watts
First published in 2022 by
The Watts Publishing Group

Text © Franklin Watts 2022
Illustrations © Trevor Dunton 2022

The right of Trevor Dunton to be identified as the illustrator
of this Work has been asserted in accordance with the
Copyright, Designs and Patents Act, 1988.

Editor: Jackie Hamley
Designer: Cathryn Gilbert and Peter Scoulding

A CIP catalogue record for this book is available
from the British Library.

ISBN 978 1 4451 7991 9 (hardback)
ISBN 978 1 4451 7992 6 (paperback)
ISBN 978 1 4451 8370 1 (ebook)

Printed in China

Franklin Watts
An imprint of
Hachette Children's Group
Part of The Watts Publishing Group
Carmelite House
50 Victoria Embankment
London EC4Y 0DZ

An Hachette UK company.
www.hachette.co.uk

www.hachettechildrens.co.uk

MIX
Paper from
responsible sources
FSC® C104740